Wishwhat

Alex Brychta

Oxford University Press

Oxford Toronto Melbourne

Oxford University Press, Walton Street, Oxford OX2 6DP

Oxford New York Toronto
Delhi Bombay Calcutta Madras Karachi
Petaling Jaya Singapore Hong Kong Tokyo
Nairobi Dar es Salaam Cape Town
Melbourne Auckland

and associated companies in
Berlin Ibadan

Oxford is a trade mark of Oxford University Press

British Library Cataloguing in Publication Data
Brychta, Alex
Wishwhat.
I. Title
823'. 914 [J]   PZ7

ISBN 0-19-279786-7 Hardback
ISBN 0-19-272219-0 Paperback

Phototypeset by Tradespools Ltd, Frome, Somerset
Printed in Hong Kong

Mr and Mrs Boon were quite ordinary people,
living in an ordinary house ...

in an ordinary street …

in an ordinary town.

Every afternoon, their grandson Danny stopped at their house on his way from school, to have some tea and biscuits with them.

One drizzly day, Danny looked at their lazy dog
called Ross, and said:
'I wish Ross would do some funny tricks,
instead of just sleeping.'

Suddenly, as if by magic, Ross jumped up,
and started to perform some very funny tricks.

The following afternoon, they were all getting
a bit fed up of the dog's feet tapping on the
floorboards.
'I wish we had a decent carpet on the floor …
sighed Mrs Boon.

To everyone's great surprise, a beautiful, new,
deep pile carpet appeared under their feet.

A few days later, while they were having tea again, it was stormy and dark outside. Mr Boon spilled his tea and complained:
'I can't see anything with this old lamp, I wish we had something a bit brighter …'

They couldn't believe their eyes.
A large crystal chandelier was hanging from
the ceiling.

'Now we can see how shabby our furniture is,' said Mrs Boon. 'I wish we had some nice, modern chairs and a table to go with them.'

As soon as she had finished the sentence, their old shabby furniture turned into a brand new, modern dining set.

The next day, as the three settled down to
have tea again, Danny looked around at the walls.
'It's nice and bright here,' he said, 'but I wish
the walls were a better colour, and we had some
pictures to look at …'

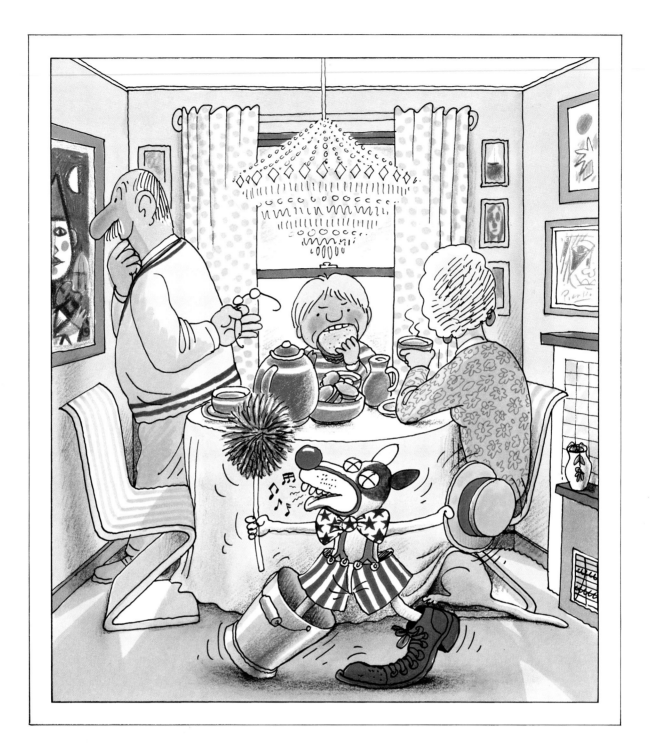

Danny's wish at once came true.
The walls were a pale cream colour, and lots
of fine paintings hung upon them.

Not long after that, on a bright sunny day,
Mr Boon looked through their small window.
'I wish we had a larger window, so we could
see more of the garden,' he said.

At that instant, they almost fell off their chairs in amazement. In place of the old sash window were enormous French windows.

'That's lovely!' exclaimed Mrs Boon. 'But look at the state of our garden. I wish we had something better to look at.'

As they watched, the back yard with its dustbins
and coal bunker, was transformed into a tiny
park, full of flowers, palms, and a fountain.

'Wonderful …' they all said together, as they
walked outside. But Mr Boon wasn't quite
satisfied. 'I wish the house looked as good as the
garden,' he said.

The three of them stood there, expecting another miracle. But nothing happened.
They checked the front of the house, but that too hadn't changed.

The following teatime, Danny had an idea.
'Perhaps wishes only come true when we are
sitting here, having tea,' he wondered. And
to test it, he called out: 'I wish the house
was as nice as the garden!'

They rushed out to look at the house.
And sure enough, it looked like a miniature
palace.

So they all went back inside very happy, and to celebrate their new discovery, they wished for a brand new set of teacups.

A week later, everything around them was new.
They drank tea, and tried very hard to think
of something else they could wish for.

Suddenly, Danny looked at the teapot.
'That's it!' he cried. 'We still have the
old teapot. I wish we had a new solid gold
teapot!'

In one bright flash, there was a beautiful,
gleaming new teapot standing in the middle
of the table.
But ...

... everything else was old again. The lamp,
the window, the garden. Even Ross went back
to sleep. They were shocked!

They filled the new pot with tea, and shouted:
'We want our old teapot back! We want everything
to be like it was before!'
But it was too late.

The magic had gone with the Wishpot.